Purr-im Cat

חתול של פורים

PITSPOPANY

NEW YORK ♦ JERUSALEM

PURR-IM CAT
by Wendy Ruth Gottlieb

Purr-im Cat
Published by Pitspopany Press

ISBN: 978-1-932687-91-0

Pitspopany Press titles may be purchased for fund raising programs
by schools and organizations by contacting:

Marketing Director, Pitspopany Press
Tel: (212) 444-1657
Fax: (866) 205-3966
Email: pitspop@netvision.net.il
Website: www.pitspopany.com

All photographs are real and were taken with Kodak 100 and 200 ASA film.

Printed in Israel

Acknowledgments

(i.e., thank you, thank you, thank you)

Thanks to Mark, Serach and Shifra
for letting me make costumes for you before I had a cat to dress up.
I am glad that you, and Seymour too, still get into the spirit of Purim
with your clever costumes and silly hats!

Thanks to Yaacov Peterseil for your invaluable writing and marketing ideas.

Thanks especially to Hashem for enabling me to have the strength, abilities and fabric
to make these costumes and quilts which are so much fun to do.

They should make them days of feasting and joy,
and of sending delicacies to one another, and gifts to the poor.
(Megillat Esther 9:22)

On Purim my cat loves to dress up for fun.
Look at Cinnamon's costumes and pick the best one.

Here is a sailor with the face of a cat,

Birthday boy - ילד היום הולדת

and a birthday boy in a party hat.

King - מלך

A king would need a golden crown.

Queen - מלכה

A queen could wear a velvet gown.

Little boy - ילד

This little boy has a ball that's red.

Little girl - ילדה

This little girl has a bear for her bed.

Fat cat - חתול שמן

A fat cat needs to stuff his shirt.

Soldier - חייל

A soldier must remain alert.

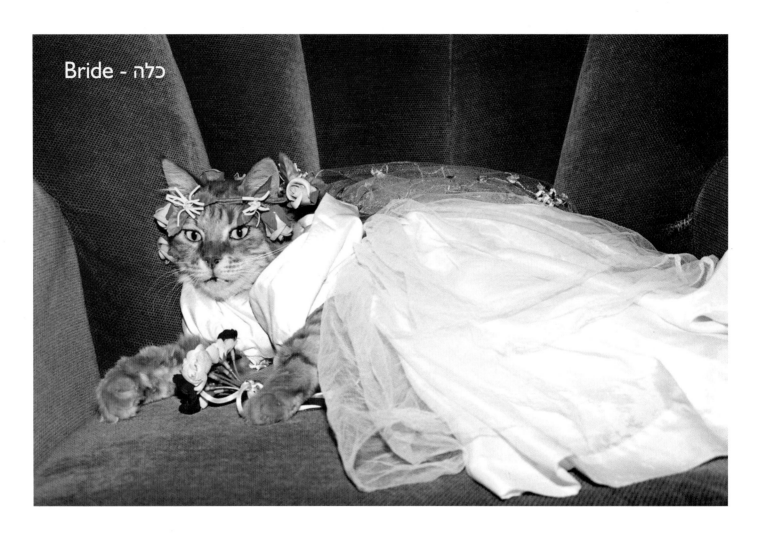

A bride in white can be real cute,

Groom - חתן

while grooms look better in a suit.

Farmer - איכר

This farmer wears blue overalls,

Superhero - גיבור

while Supercat buys his capes in the malls.

Granny - סבתא

This granny has yarn for making a sweater.

Grandpa - סבא

This grandpa holds something to help him see better.

Cat Burglar - פורץ

A burglar mask looks best at night.

Pirate - שודד-ים

A pirate needs a bird that's bright.

Rabbit - ארנבת

This rabbit's ears are really big,

Clown - ליצן

and this clown dons a colored wig.

Policeman - שוטר

A policeman hangs things from his belt loop,

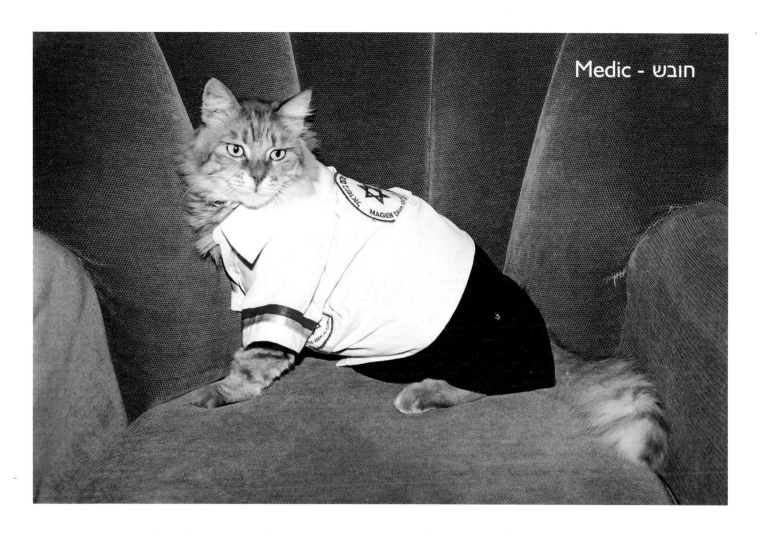

Medic - חובש

while medics cure with chicken soup.

Purim basket – משלוח מנות

A Purim basket is filled with good stuff.

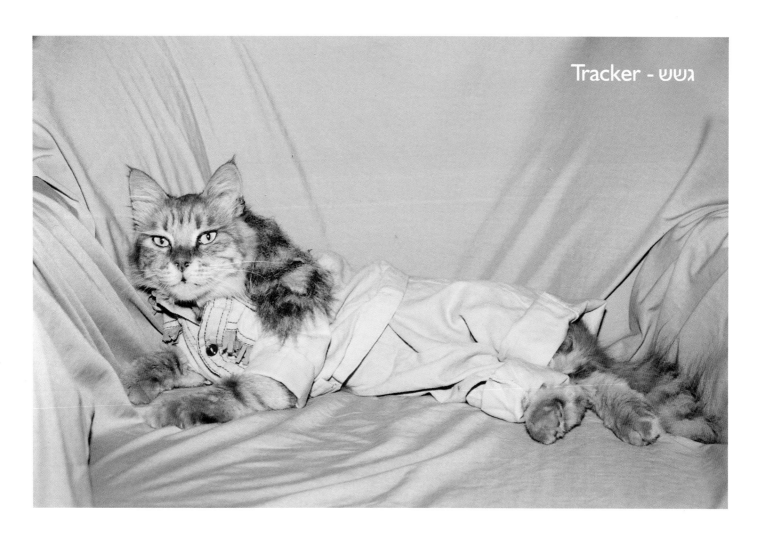

A tracker's clothes must be really tough.

Baby doll - בובה

A baby doll loves bottles and bows,

Sleepyhead - ישנוני

while sleepyheads' PJ's cover their toes.

If you are little or you are big,

you can wear a costume, or just wear a wig.

On Purim no matter what you do,
just make sure your costume fits you!